*To the kid who peers into the night sky with
a heart full of wonder . . . this is for you.*
—KCB

*To my sister, Patti,
who with her tremendous sense of humor
has saved me from a few black holes.*
—Deborah

*A supermassive thank you to Fabio Pacucci
and the Black Hole Initiative for ensuring I
got my facts straight, even when they bent my
brain. You all do great work, and I anxiously
await your next big discovery.* —KCB

SLEEPING BEAR PRESS™

Text Copyright © 2022 Keri Claiborne Boyle
Illustration Copyright © 2022 Deborah Melmon
Design Copyright © 2022 Sleeping Bear Press
All inquiries should be addressed to:
Sleeping Bear Press
2395 South Huron Parkway, Suite 200
Ann Arbor, MI 48104
www.sleepingbearpress.com © Sleeping Bear Press

Printed and bound in the United States
10 9 8 7 6 5 4 3 2 1
ISBN: 978-1-53411-152-3
Library of Congress Cataloging-in-Publication Data on file.

THE BLACK HOLE DEBACLE

Keri Claiborne Boyle

Illustrated by
Deborah Melmon

PUBLISHED BY SLEEPING BEAR PRESS™

Jordie's future as an astronomer was written in the stars.

She was awed by asteroids,

perplexed by planets,

and mesmerized by moons.

JORDIE

She'd even named her dog Neptune.

So when something out-of-this-world happened in the middle of Ms. Snoreburger's geography lesson, Jordie couldn't believe her luck. . . .

There, churning in Jordie's desk, was a black hole.

She reached in for a pencil, but the black hole got to it first.

She reached in for crayons, but it gobbled them up too.

SLURP

She reached in for her latest *Mission to Mars* magazines, but they were gone in one ginormous gulp.

Jordie stopped reaching in. After all,
something capable of noshing planets might like hand sandwiches too.

Fortunately, Jordie's class seemed unaware of the shadowy stranger.

No one would let her keep a hungry black hole.
And Jordie was definitely going to keep it.

Given the gravity of the situation, the black hole would have to remain a secret.

While class droned on, Jordie watched the black hole
swallow her lunch box, pencil case, and geography homework—
to Ms. Snoreburger's annoyance.

She didn't really have a choice.
It's not like you can scold a black hole
for its less-than-stellar manners.

After school, Jordie used her left rain boot to coax the black hole
into her backpack. There, it snarfed down her water bottle,
library books, and the softball glove Molly had lent her.

Now Molly refused to sit next to Jordie on the bus!

What could Jordie say? That at least the black hole hadn't snacked on Molly instead?

At home, Jordie shooed Neptune away and crammed the black hole into her closet. Of course, it promptly gorged on her soccer ball, sweatshirt, unicorn underwear, and favorite pom-pom hat.

It did, however, spit back the unicorn underwear.

At dinner, when Jordie asked to replace some of her "lost" items,
she got a stern lecture about "being more responsible" with her belongings.
Now Ms. Snoreburger, Molly, and Jordie's parents were mad at her.

If only the black hole preferred broccoli and meat loaf
over softball gloves and geography homework.

Things were definitely getting tricky.

Grrrrr...

Meanwhile, back in Jordie's room,
things had gone from tricky to troublesome. . . .

The black hole had gotten bigger and was now spilling out of her closet.

Then the situation went from troublesome to terrible. . . .

The voracious visitor began pulling things off her shelves and drinking the light!
A soccer trophy whizzed past Jordie's head as the room grew dimmer.

Then things went from terrible to truly tragic....

On the floor . . . in the middle of her room . . . lay Neptune's empty collar.

"Did you eat my dog?!" Jordie shouted into the void.

BURP

In response, the black hole let
out a polite burp.

Feasting on pom-pom hats and sweatshirts was one thing,
devouring her dog was another!

Jordie slammed her door shut and paced in the hallway, trying to
formulate a plan. She didn't know what would happen to Neptune, but
she did know that nothing could escape an ordinary black hole—not even light.

But then, this was no ordinary black hole.

She had to get her dog back.

Jordie opened her door to find that the black hole now filled her entire room. She took a deep breath, stepped to the black hole's edge, and leapt into its shadowy center.

Jordie tumbled in a darkness that seemed to grow colder and colder.

She could feel the black hole's gravity stretching her body into a long, thin noodle.

And when she opened her mouth to holler for Neptune,

no sound came out.

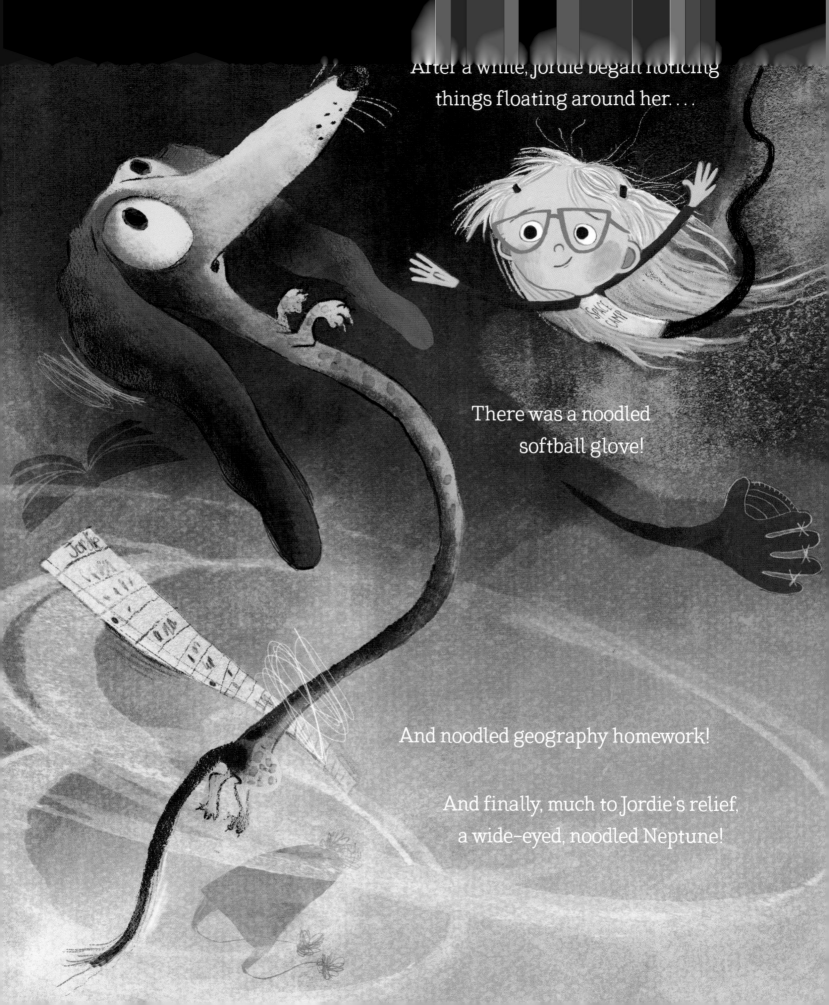

After a while, Jordie began noticing things floating around her. . . .

There was a noodled softball glove!

And noodled geography homework!

And finally, much to Jordie's relief, a wide-eyed, noodled Neptune!

Jordie snatched Neptune, the glove, and—
to make Ms. Snoreburger happy—her homework.

Then, she reached deep into her pocket and pulled out . . .

the unicorn underwear.

PATOOOEY!

The next thing Jordie knew, she was sprawled on the floor
with a whimpering, now un-noodled Neptune licking her face.

Jordie sat up and considered her cosmic acquaintance,
who was now seeping into the hall.

She'd had quite an adventure, but Jordie knew—black holes needed space.

They were meant to graze galaxies and slurp stars, not dine on dogs.

So, while her parents watched TV, Jordie used one of her rainbow sneakers to entice the black hole out into her yard. There, after one last wistful look, she firmly kicked it into the night sky.

The next morning, Jordie slumped at her desk.
Her rescue mission had really stretched her thin.

But when she reached in for a pencil,
she found her desk jam-packed.

Slowly, Jordie pulled out a water bottle, sweatshirt,
pencil case, lunch box, soccer ball, her left rain boot,
a pom-pom hat, pencil, crayons, and one
rainbow sneaker.

Only her library books and
magazines were missing.

Why Jordie's galactic guest had ventured into her desk in the first place would remain a mystery.

But now, Jordie knew something that no other astronomer knew....

It turns out, black holes
are ravenous readers.

The Black Hole: Space's Most Mysterious Monster

For a long time, black holes were just a theory—or an unproven idea. No one knew if they actually existed. Their modern-day discovery began in 1915, when theoretical physicist Albert Einstein created a complicated, mind-bending mathematical theory in an attempt to explain how energy, matter, space, and time interacted—it was called the Theory of General Relativity. But even though his theory allowed for the existence of black holes, the concept was so bizarre that Einstein himself refused to believe it!

But then, by applying Einstein's theory, theorist Karl Schwarzschild discovered that gravity could indeed warp space and time around dense, spherical objects—like a planet or star—creating a "hole" in space and time. Since then, scientists have tried to find black holes by observing the movement of stars and planets around them. Still, black holes were just a theory . . . until this theory finally became a reality. In 2019, a team of scientists captured the first-ever image of a supermassive black hole by linking nine radio telescopes across the globe to create a virtual, Earth-sized observatory called the Event Horizon Telescope.

Where Do Black Holes Come From?

Black holes are usually created when a massive star runs out of fuel and dies a violent death. Its immense gravity causes the core of the star to collapse on itself, creating a "rip" in space and time. The black hole's gravity is so strong that it pulls in everything that comes too close. And once something crosses the event horizon, it can never escape—including light! Many space scientists believe that our own Milky Way galaxy contains millions—even billions!—of black holes. And though they can move rapidly through space, we're fortunate there are no black holes too close to us . . . if one were to wander through our solar system, it could eat our planet!

What Would Happen if You Fell Into a Black Hole?

No one knows for sure since the closest black hole to Earth is thought to be about 3,000 light years away. Still, it's safe to say that things would get very weird. Because gravity can alter time and space, time would slow down as you got closer to the black hole. You wouldn't notice it, but to someone observing from afar, it'd look as if you were barely moving. Then, once you crossed over the event horizon—an experience you probably wouldn't survive—the black hole's immense gravity would smoosh you into a teeny-tiny dot when you finally reached its center. But not before you were "spaghettified" along the way. This is exactly what it sounds like . . . you'd be stretched into a long, thin noodle. Pasta, anyone?

Are Black Holes Big? It's All Relative....

On the small side, a black hole might only be a few miles across with a mass of 2 to 3 times the mass of our sun. Other black holes are so astronomically large, they're hard to comprehend: billions of miles wide with a mass of 10 billion or more suns! The supermassive black hole at the center of our own galaxy is about 4 million times the mass of our sun.

There's much more to learn about black holes and scientists continue to study their strange behavior. Someday, a better understanding of these galactic neighbors may just help unlock the secrets of our amazing and awe-inspiring universe.

Want to Know More About Black Holes?

Visit the Black Hole Initiative (BHI) at bhi.fas.harvard.edu and NASA at nasa.gov.